I Have a Dream ...

Written by Levi David Addai
Illustrated by Qi Debrah

CHARACTERS

Raheem Harris

Teresa Harris

Martin Luther King, Jr

Yolanda King

I HAVE A DREAM ...

SCENE 1

Atlanta, August, 1963

(Martin Luther King, Jr is in his study. There's a knock at the door.)

MARTIN: Come in.

(Enter Yolanda.)

MARTIN: It's way past your bedtime.

YOLANDA: But I can't sleep.

MARTIN: That's not my problem.

YOLANDA: I promise I won't make any noise.
Just five minutes.

MARTIN: But you know how busy I am
right now …

YOLANDA: I know, I know, and that's why
I'll be reeeeeal quiet.

3

MARTIN:	Look, come in properly before you wake up your brothers and sister.
YOLANDA:	What's that you're working on?
MARTIN:	My speech for when we're on the Lincoln Memorial steps.
YOLANDA:	Oh. So you haven't finished it yet?
MARTIN:	No, it's not easy trying to write a speech that you know will have the ears of America listening …
YOLANDA:	What have you written so far?
MARTIN:	I thought you were going to be quiet.
YOLANDA:	But since I'm here, I may as well make myself useful.

MARTIN: All right, all right. *(clears his throat and begins to read a section)*

"I have a vision today. A vision so clear and so bold. A vision so sweet and so rich. A vision so dense and so strong. A vision …"

YOLANDA: What's with all the "visions"?

MARTIN: Oh, a vision is … foresight … prophesy … imagination of what's to come.

YOLANDA: That's a boring word.

MARTIN: Right, bed. I need to get this speech written. Come on Yolanda, you know how important the next few days are. Do you know how many people are involved in this demonstration? Do you know how many months of planning and even how many years – no, decades – our people have waited for an opportunity like this?

YOLANDA: I … I just get … scared sometimes. Suppose … you get arrested again?

MARTIN: Then once again the police will be arresting an innocent man – that will no doubt further promote our fight for equality.

YOLANDA: What if some racists start a riot?

MARTIN: Then we will continue to counter with non-violent means, so that we're set apart from the troublemakers.

YOLANDA: But what if it gets real violent – and you get hurt … real bad … like … killed?

MARTIN: Well, honey … life ain't no crystal stair. Every generation has somebody that sometimes has to make the ultimate sacrifice in order for people to get to the next level. But I'm prepared to make that sacrifice, if it means a better future for America and, of course, you my dear.

YOLANDA: Don't talk like that Dad. I need you.

MARTIN: And I need you and America to have a better future,
where it doesn't judge citizens by the colour of their skin.
This speech needs to be heard and understood not just by
black folk but white folk, Jews, Latinos, Asians,
Native Americans and everyone else in-between.
My speech will be for all of them.

7

YOLANDA: Still think you can use a better word than "vision".

MARTIN: *(laughs)* Yes, miss. I have a meeting with my speech writing team tomorrow evening and I'll see what they suggest.

YOLANDA: You don't need them Dad. They'll just give you more boring words to send people to sleep.

MARTIN: Just because a word might not sound exciting, doesn't mean it can't be powerful and even change the world! And there is a vast amount of people who, like us, want change. They hope for change, pray about change, eat change, drink change, sleep change and dream about change.

YOLANDA: I like the word "dream" better.

MARTIN: As do I. And do you know what else dreams are associated with?

(Yolanda shakes her head.)

MARTIN: Sleep! So get to bed.

(Martin Luther King, Jr goes back to writing his speech. Yolanda sighs and exits.)

9

SCENE 2

London, 2013

(Raheem enters the living room, followed by a disappointed Teresa holding his exercise book.)

TERESA: So, are you going to tell me what the meaning of all this is?

(Raheem shrugs his shoulders.)

TERESA: So you have nothing to say?

(Again, Raheem shrugs his shoulders.)

TERESA: Look at these grades! How can this be happening under my nose?

(Again, Raheem shrugs his shoulders.)

TERESA: You think I enjoy hearing my colleague complaining about your nonsense?

(Raheem shakes his head.)

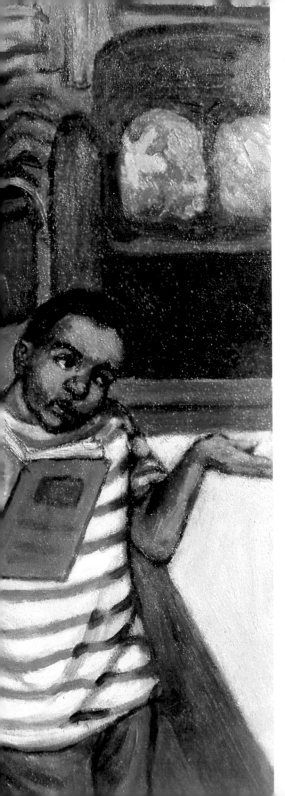

TERESA:	And why am I again hearing that you're distracting other pupils from learning?
RAHEEM:	Kieron, Leon, Marlon always sit at my table, so ...
TERESA:	Why don't you move tables, like I've told you to several times!
RAHEEM:	I do, but they follow me!
TERESA:	Really? So wherever you go, they follow like sheep?
RAHEEM:	Yeah. And then they spend the whole day just cracking jokes.
TERESA:	And what do you do when they're "cracking jokes"?
RAHEEM:	Laugh! *(chuckles)* They're funny, man.

11

TERESA:	So this is all some sort of joke to you?
RAHEEM:	No, Mum.
TERESA:	I've never been so embarrassed. Did you even think how your actions might reflect on me? How can I be teaching other children when I can't control my own? It's embarrassing! And what was the meaning of this?
RAHEEM:	It was just some Black History project.
TERESA:	An important History project! All you had to do was write your own "I have a dream" speech but what did you do, Raheem? What type of nonsense is this?
RAHEEM:	But Mum, they're not all bad. I did write about other more ... serious dreams.
TERESA:	What, like the dream about *(looking at essay)* "time-travelling" or the dream of being "rich and famous"?
RAHEEM:	But I do wanna be rich and famous.

(Teresa sighs.)

TERESA:	You know what? You can go to your room – I haven't got the patience for this right now.
RAHEEM:	If I was Reece Smith or Ryan Collins you wouldn't be coming heavy like this, but because I'm Raheem Harris, son of Ms Harris, teacher of 4A, I get it worst!

TERESA:	Well, I'm sorry to inform you Raheem that life ain't no crystal stair! And what about your secondary school application? *(picking up the application form)* Do you even care about your future?
RAHEEM:	Yeah, of course.
TERESA:	Because all I've heard today is how you muck around and won't do what Miss Wallace asks. *(waving Raheem's exercise book)* And as for this, this should have been easy! I should be hearing that you got an A star or something!

RAHEEM:	What? 'Cos it was about Martin Luther King? I'm fed up of hearing about that guy, man.
TERESA:	Why?
RAHEEM:	'Cos he got shot dead! He's got nothing to do with my life or anything.
TERESA:	But look how many stories I've told you about him. I've shown you how his work helped bring change to the world.
RAHEEM:	Yeah, his world in the stone-aged years. It's useless. What's the point of learning about it?
TERESA:	*(horrified)* What's the point?
RAHEEM:	I can't be bothered with that, man. It's boring, he's boring.
TERESA:	Do you know what my dream was, when I was your age?
RAHEEM:	I bet it was to do with something boring, like being a teacher.
TERESA:	You're right, it was.
RAHEEM:	I knew it!
TERESA:	But I got there didn't I? And you know how?
RAHEEM:	Nope.
TERESA:	Through hard work.
RAHEEM:	I don't wanna be a teacher.

TERESA:	I didn't say you have to be. I'm just curious to know what your dream is Raheem. It might help you … focus more.
RAHEEM:	Well, I gave an answer, but you ruled it out so I guess I don't have one.
TERESA:	But you see, if you don't have a dream, how you gonna have a dream come true?
RAHEEM:	What am I – five? Gosh! Life ain't like a Disney film, man. Dreams don't come true. They're just … dreams.
TERESA:	Oh really?
RAHEEM:	And you being a teacher doesn't count.
TERESA:	OK, Mr Cynical. But, what if I was to tell you that my new dream is to become the head teacher at your school?
RAHEEM:	Huh? Are you serious? You can't do that!
TERESA:	Why not? It's my dream.
RAHEEM:	But … but … what about me?
TERESA:	I've been a teacher at your school for how many years now and you've been fine. Nothing's going to change.
RAHEEM:	It will! This is so unfair!
TERESA:	No, what would be unfair would be me not being able to apply for the job in the first place.
RAHEEM:	Why would they stop you?

TERESA: Because there was a time when people that looked like you and me weren't allowed to do certain things, at least not with everyone else. But people like Martin Luther King fought hard so that I could be treated the same.

RAHEEM: Here we go again.

TERESA: I'm not ashamed to say Dr Martin Luther King, Jr is my hero. And do you know why?

(Teresa goes to get a book about Martin Luther King and holds it up. Raheem sighs.)

TERESA: This man had a dream of a united America …

RAHEEM: And got killed for it.

TERESA: Yes, he paid the ultimate price for wanting freedom and equality for all Americans.

RAHEEM: Again, with America! But what's that got to do with me
            in London?

TERESA: What you need to understand, Raheem, is that there was
            a time when there was a lot of segregation in the world …
            people were segregated because of their race.

RAHEEM: Like a 100 metres race? (laughs)

TERESA:	*(stern)* RAHEEM! I've had enough of your backchat. And you can forget about your computer games, you're banned from playing them for a month.
RAHEEM:	What?
TERESA:	I'm gonna put a stop to this behaviour before it goes too far!

(Teresa hands to Raheem the Martin Luther King book.)

20

TERESA: Read this out loud from the beginning. I'm going to put dinner on.

RAHEEM: *(sighs)* Not again.

TERESA: It's your own fault!

(Teresa exits leaving the door open. Raheem begins to read the book, mumbling his way through.)

RAHEEM: *(reading from book)* "Dr Martin Luther King, Jr was born on the 15th January 1929 in Atlanta, Georgia, the United States of America ..."

(Raheem yawns. His eyes get heavier. The room is now pitch black, suddenly he lands in Yolanda's bedroom – 1963. Yolanda enters the room.)

RAHEEM: Who are you?

YOLANDA: I'm Yolanda, Yolanda King, and you are trespassing in my bedroom.

RAHEEM: And where is your bedroom?

YOLANDA: In my house.

RAHEEM: What's with all the riddles, man. Just give me a straight answer.

YOLANDA: You give me a straight answer mister!

RAHEEM: Am I even in London?

YOLANDA: London, England?

RAHEEM: Derr! Where else?

23

YOLANDA: You're in Atlanta, Georgia!

RAHEEM: America? This place doesn't look ... right. What year is it?

YOLANDA: 1963.

RAHEEM: 1963?

YOLANDA: Yes – 1.9.6.3!

RAHEEM: Right, OK ... erm ... Yolanda King, you say?

(Yolanda nods.)

RAHEEM: Daughter of Martin Luther King?

(Yolanda nods again.)

RAHEEM: OK then ... I'm just gonna go and erm ... I'm just gonna ... sit down for a moment ... Oh my days!

SCENE 3

(Raheem sleeps on the floor with his head resting on a teddy bear and his body covered with a sheet. Yolanda enters the room with a hot drink and creeps up to him.)

YOLANDA: Wakey-wakey, sleepyhead.

RAHEEM: *(turning over, groaning)* I don't want to go to school today, Mum.

YOLANDA: *(offended)* Hey, do I look like ya mom, sleepyhead?

RAHEEM: Oh no, I'm still dreaming, I gotta wake up!

(Raheem begins to slap his face but Yolanda stops him.)

YOLANDA: Calm down ... calm down! Here, I managed to sneak some hot chocolate for you. Now tell me how you got here.

RAHEEM: I don't know. I was getting told off because of the bad mark I got for my Black History project – just because I don't know much about the "civil fights".

YOLANDA: Civil what?

RAHEEM: The "civil fights movement". You know, the whole thing about black people in America.

YOLANDA: Civil rights!

RAHEEM: Yeah, that's what I meant.

YOLANDA: *(laughs to herself)* "Civil fights".

RAHEEM: Well, all that stuff happened in America a long, long time ago. It's got nothing to do with me.

YOLANDA: You'll be surprised just how much of that "stuff" relates to you Raheem Martin Harris. It's obvious you've been sent here to learn a thing or two.

(Raheem sighs.)

YOLANDA: *(looking at Raheem's book)* So you've heard of Reverend Doctor Martin Luther King, Junior, but have you heard of ... Rosa Parks?

(Raheem shakes his head.)

YOLANDA: Harriet Tubman?

(Raheem shakes his head.)

YOLANDA: Abraham Lincoln?

(Raheem shakes his head.)

YOLANDA: You haven't heard of Abraham Lincoln? Hang on.

(Yolanda pulls out a giant world map that covers her floor.)

YOLANDA: Now, I don't wanna be up all night so let's do this. Now, for you to fully understand why my father's important, you'll need to have a basic understanding of history, of how the world ended up being how it is in my time in 1963, before you go forward to your time. Now go to Africa.

RAHEEM: That's easy.

(Raheem walks to Africa, Yolanda stands on Europe.)

YOLANDA: Right, in the time where we begin, Europeans have already discovered what they call the "New World" – naming it?

RAHEEM: Erm … Earth the second?

YOLANDA: America!

RAHEEM: *(lies)* Oh yeah, I knew that. *(points)* That's there, innit?

YOLANDA: Hold both your arms out towards me.

RAHEEM: Why?

YOLANDA: Don't question, just do it.

(Raheem sighs and holds his arms out.)

YOLANDA: Now, some Europeans thought they needed ... "help"
building the New World. So they travelled from Europe ...

(Yolanda walks on the map from Europe to Africa.)

YOLANDA: To Africa and took people there ...

(Yolanda takes out two scarves and ties Raheem's wrists and ankles together.)

YOLANDA: As their slaves. Now, pretend these are handcuffs.

RAHEEM: Hey, what have I done?

YOLANDA: Exactly … exactly. Now …

(Yolanda leads Raheem across the Atlantic Ocean to America.)

YOLANDA: … The Europeans took the African slaves to the Americas. Some went to South American countries such as Brazil, some went to Caribbean countries like Jamaica …

RAHEEM: That's where my Nan's from.

YOLANDA: And some went to the United States, where they were treated horribly. All that the slaves had was their faith and a dream that one day they'd be free. And then a few hundred years later, Abraham Lincoln became President. Now Abe Lincoln believed "that all men are created equal" – including slaves.

RAHEEM: Cool.

(Raheem walks over to Yolanda and offers his handcuffed wrists for release, but she stops him.)

YOLANDA: BUT certain Southern states didn't like his idea of slaves being free, so war broke out between the South and the North. During the Civil War, Abe Lincoln announced the "Emancipation Proclamation", which meant that all slaves in the entire United States were now free. And a couple of years later, the North had finally won the war and so the slaves in the South were also …

(Yolanda brings Raheem over to the "North" and unshackles his wrists.)

YOLANDA: … free. It was only a few days after that, that … Abe Lincoln was killed.

(Raheem goes to walk, but stumbles on to the floor. He remembers his ankles are still shackled.)

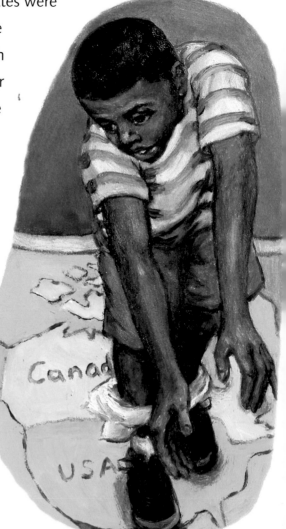

RAHEEM: I can't walk properly!

YOLANDA: Why not? You're not a slave anymore, you're free!

RAHEEM: *(points to his ankles)* Derr! The handcuffs ...

YOLANDA: Exactly – the handcuffs! In the 1860s, Abraham Lincoln declared African Americans free, but a hundred years later here in 1963, yes we might be free by law, but the handcuffs of injustice that stop African Americans from getting jobs and having the freedom and the same rights as everyone else, still remain.

RAHEEM: Wow, you certainly know your stuff.

YOLANDA: *(smug)* I get it from my dad. Have you read any of his speeches? Of course not, what am I saying? You don't even care.

RAHEEM: I have! I've got no choice with my mum, she's got books galore. She's always going on about him.

YOLANDA: Well, if you're telling the truth, you'll know that my father is one of the leaders of what some people call the "civil rights movement". He's leading a march in Washington in two days' time to help get the handcuffs off *(takes off the scarf around Raheem's ankles)*. There's gonna be a march right under President Kennedy's nose. Some people say there's gonna be thousands there marching. There'll be speeches and songs, all on the steps of the Lincoln Memorial.

RAHEEM: What's that?

YOLANDA: It's this place in Washington containing all things Abraham
            Lincoln. But what's really amazing is that there's this huge,
            and I mean massive, statue of President Lincoln outside,
            (demonstrates) sitting on a chair looking … presidential.
            You do remember who President Abraham Lincoln is,
            don't you?

RAHEEM: Yeah, he's the one who announced, erm … promised
            conversations?

YOLANDA: Emancipation proclamation! And what did that mean?

RAHEEM: It meant that the slaves were free. But they weren't
            totally free because they were still being treated unfairly.
            Lincoln got killed and all these years later black people still
            can't get jobs and that, so now your dad and a bunch of
            others are going to Washington to march about it. OK, I've
            learnt my lesson, now can I please go home?

(Yolanda looks sad.)

RAHEEM: Hey, I didn't mean it in a bad way. Just saying I've been here
            a while now and my mum must be wondering where I am.
            What's up? You shouldn't be sad. Remember who your
            dad is? I wish I had a famous dad.

YOLANDA: No you don't.

RAHEEM: Yeah man, it would be cool. I'd get to travel all over the placc, mcct famous pcoplc. I bct you cvcn gct to mcct thc President and that.

YOLANDA: What does your dad do, Raheem?

RAHEEM: I don't know. He's ... not around.

YOLANDA: Oh ...

RAHEEM: But I wouldn't be complaining if he was around. Especially if he was famous!

YOLANDA: But that's the thing. My dad is famous for having this, this – big dream for America and that's all he ever goes on about. "Changing America", "Praying for America", "Shaking America", "Uniting America", America, America, America – but what about me?

RAHEEM: What about you?

YOLANDA: I've never heard him speak about me like he does about America.

RAHEEM:	Don't mean he doesn't care or even have a dream for your future.
YOLANDA:	Don't you lecture me about dreams and the future, that's my job!
RAHEEM:	Huh?
YOLANDA:	That's the very reason why you were sent back here. You live in your 21st-century world with every job and ambition at your fingertips but instead, what do you do? Play video games, play video games and play more video games!
RAHEEM:	*(laughs)* That pretty much sums up my free time.
YOLANDA:	This is not a joke, Raheem! Do you know what my generation would do if we had even a fraction of the opportunities you guys have in the future?
RAHEEM:	I dunno. Play video games?
YOLANDA:	You were sent back here so I could shape you up and make you realise how important it is to have a dream. So I want you to write down your dream. What do you want to do in life? What's important to you?
RAHEEM:	Ah man. This is like schoolwork and you're not my teacher!
YOLANDA:	Hey, this is 1963, you're not even born yet, so I make the rules around here, OK? Now get to it!

SCENE 4

(Yolanda sits reading and marking Raheem's work, tutting as she goes along. Raheem watches her.)

RAHEEM: You're not marking it for spelling, are you?

YOLANDA: No, I'm not marking it for spelling, though I do feel for the teachers in your time. But all of this here – this doesn't tell me what you want to do in life.

RAHEEM: Excuse me for being ten years old and not having my whole life planned out.

37

YOLANDA: I'm not saying it should be planned out, but you must appreciate the freedom you have in your time. Do you?

RAHEEM: … Yeah.

YOLANDA: You don't sound too convincing.

RAHEEM: It's just different in my time.

YOLANDA: There are so many important things that you can do for yourself and other people. Take a look around you, see what's taking place here. People in my time are fighting with everything they've got so that we, as black people, can be seen and treated as human beings. You wanna be a "footballer" or "singer" or "dancer", that's fine, but then let it be a dream that you put everything into, that you won't take for granted. Because in your time, there's never been a better time in history for your dreams to come true.

RAHEEM: *(sighs to himself)* Here we go again.

YOLANDA: What's wrong?

RAHEEM: That last bit. My mum tells me the same thing over and over again.

YOLANDA: *(stern)* That's because it's true. Now, I want you to tell me your dream. You might not have an exact idea of a job but tell me what you hope for, where you would like to be in the future.

RAHEEM: So, what is my dream? My dream is for world peace. People need to stop fighting each other, man. Erm ... also, people need to be treated fairly and the same, it doesn't matter who they are or what they look like. Everyone should be treated equally. Except the Queen, 'cos she's – the Queen. And the President, 'cos he's – the President. I guess you could add the Prime Minister to that list as well. Anyway, all people should be treated equally. Except for royal people, presidents and prime ministers – it's no use man, I'm not Shakespeare, I can't do it, I'm rubbish.

YOLANDA: You don't have to be a writer to be able to express how you feel.

RAHEEM: Ah, that's easy for you to say. You see your dad do it all the time, at church, in marches. And Americans in general, they're known for being loud and all shouty. I'm British, we don't talk.

YOLANDA: So I guess you Brits just communicate by blinking or something then?

RAHEEM: No ...

YOLANDA: Or speaking really quietly, like a church mouse, afraid to be heard.

RAHEEM: Nah, man – we just don't get all militant like you lot, with all the marches.

YOLANDA: Is that right?

RAHEEM: Yeah, man. I mean, you never hear any stories of black people in Britain demonstrating and that.

YOLANDA: (laughs to herself) Your country has had its fair share of demonstrations.

RAHEEM: But what I mean is … black people in Britain don't have any real history – not like you lot in America. We didn't have a "Martin Luther King" or an "Abraham Lincoln". I'm sure there was probably the odd slave in Britain over time, but most black people came after World War Two. What do they call it again … Windmill … Wind tunnel … no … Windrush … Yeah, Windrush – that's it!

YOLANDA: So you really believe there weren't any important black British people?

RAHEEM: Not before 1990 … *(unsure)* 80 … 70 … well, not before World War Two!

YOLANDA: What do you know about – Ignatius Sancho?

(Raheem remains silent.)

YOLANDA: Ignatius Sancho – once dubbed "the extraordinary
            black man". He was the first black Brit to have his written
            work published. He done newspapers, plays, poems,
            composed music. But you know what else he done, beside
            all his wealth of God-given talent, huh? That same Ignatius
            Sancho was the first – black – British – man – ever … to
            vote in a UK election. The year was 1774!

RAHEEM: (surprised) Wow, I was far out. Was it really that long ago?

YOLANDA: What do you know about – Olaudah Equiano?

RAHEEM: Nothing at all.

YOLANDA: Olaudah Equiano was also known as Gustavus Vassa. Here was a man who took pen to paper and wrote a detailed account of everything he went through, from slavery to freedom. This account was so moving that it affected many who were in charge during that time and played an important and active role in the abolition of slavery in Britain. In what year was his book published? 1789!

RAHEEM: Seriously?

YOLANDA: Mary Seacole! A valiant nurse who saved and used her own money to go to the Crimean War and set up a hospital to tend to the sick, all because she wasn't allowed to look after the sick at home in England. What year did this happen? 1855!

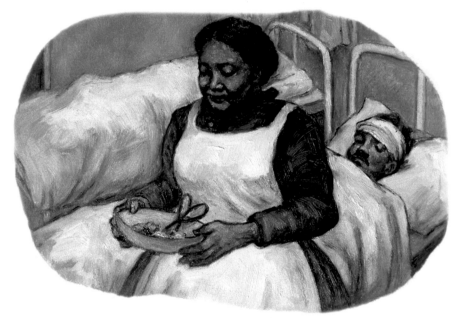

RAHEEM: Ah, man. But all these people, they're all involved with politics and hospital stuff. How was I gonna know about them?

YOLANDA: OK, here's one you should know then. Who was the first black British soccer player?

RAHEEM: There hasn't been one. But if you're asking about the first black British footballer ...

YOLANDA: *(sarcastic)* Ha-ha.

RAHEEM: I dunno – er … Rio Ferdinand?

YOLANDA: Wrong!

RAHEEM: Well, I dunno those things …

YOLANDA: Andrew Watson was the first black player to play for Scotland; Arthur Wharton, the first black professional. In what years did these moments take place? 1881 and 1889.

RAHEEM: *(impressed)* Really? Wow! I never really knew there was so much … "black stuff" going on back then. That's so cool.

YOLANDA:	Right, I want you to come up and tell me your dream.
RAHEEM:	Shouldn't I write it down first?
YOLANDA:	No, just speak from the heart.
RAHEEM:	I ... I ... I ...
YOLANDA:	Don't be shy Raheem. Just speak from the heart!

(Raheem clears his throat again.)

RAHEEM: I have a dream ... that whatever I end up doing when I'm older, I will not only be able to help myself, but help others ... like my mum. I have a dream that ... I will never take for granted what people have done in this time, and before, so that I can dream any dream I want. I have a dream that ... All my dreams will come true. I have a dream that ... Yolanda will see what her dad is doing is as much for her as it is for America. I hated the fact that my mum was a teacher at my school, and now wants to be head teacher. The idea made me ... shiver. But she's living her dream. And it's thanks to people like your father that she can.

But what about me? I'm only ten. I live in London, where I'm lucky enough to have a home and food every day. I get to watch TV, play games and just … live. But is that my fault? I wasn't born in the 1800s or the 1960s, but somehow I must carry on a … torch that I didn't light. I must take the baton, for a race I never entered. And in my time, the pressures of being fashionable, funny and famous surround me every day, in school, in newspapers and on TV. And my mum's a teacher and now wants to be head teacher. And I'm her son – so surely I must be the best behaved student, get all the best grades, be the best at everything, because my mum's a teacher.

But it ain't like that, man. And it's not because I don't know the answers, or hate school. I just don't like having the pressure of trying to live up to what others have done in the past. That's impossible. I gotta be me – like you said. I can learn all I can about the past, but what point is there if I don't find something about the past that can help me with my future? Even if the point is to help me be a better person. If everyone used History lessons to learn and make themselves a better person, then surely that would make a better world?

Abe Lincoln learnt from America's past and wanted to change its future. Your dad learnt from the past and in Washington people will hear his hopes for a better future. And this is what I can hope for in my life, even though the thought of growing up and having to do all those ... "adult things" scares me. But as long as I'm not made to feel ... small by history, I can learn from it and hopefully bring a change ... a good change, to my future. And I'll be doing my bit in changing the world – for the good ... I hope.

(Yolanda stands opened-mouthed in amazement at the speech Raheem has pulled off. Yolanda gives Raheem a big hug. Raheem is embarrassed.)

49

YOLANDA: That was just a thank-you hug.

RAHEEM: What for?

YOLANDA: For passing the test! You've inspired me Raheem. Now, I've gotta get to bed. You can sleep over there if you want.

RAHEEM: In my time, a lot of your father's dreams have come true. Not all, but the world's slowly getting there. Oh yeah, and do you know, in America they even have a public holiday called "Martin Luther King Day".

YOLANDA: Martin Luther King Day? What happened for him to get that?

RAHEEM: Erm ... I dunno. I guess you'll just have to wait and see. The whole world will be talking about what happens in Washington, and your father's life. Just don't forget to remind him to talk about his dream. You hear what I said Yolanda? Yolanda?

(Raheem turns around to see that Yolanda has disappeared. The room turns pitch black. Raheem finds himself floating through space.)

SCENE 5

(Raheem awakes back in 2013. His mother Teresa stands over him.)

RAHEEM: Mum?

TERESA: *(stern)* Wake up, Raheem!

(Raheem frantically looks around.)

RAHEEM: Yolanda?

TERESA: Who's Yolanda?

RAHEEM: Erm ... erm ... nobody ...

TERESA: So you conveniently fell asleep while reading.

RAHEEM: Did I?

51

(Teresa goes towards the kitchen.)

TERESA: Go wash your hands, dinner's ready.

RAHEEM: Mum?

TERESA: Yes, Raheem?

RAHEEM: Er ... sorry for not listening earlier.

TERESA: *(disbelieving)* Are you?

RAHEEM: Seriously – I am sorry.

TERESA: OK, but you're still in trouble.

RAHEEM: That's cool, I understand and I have no complaints.

TERESA: *(confused)* What?

RAHEEM: And by the way, I hope you get the head teacher job – you deserve it!

TERESA: Wait ... what's all this? Is there more stuff I should know about your behaviour in school?

RAHEEM: No, I had this ... dream ... but I'm not sure if it was a "dream" dream.

TERESA: What happened?

RAHEEM: Well, I went back in time to 1963. And there I met Yolanda King, Martin Luther King's oldest child. And back there I learnt about how people like Martin Luther King worked so hard, so that in our time, our dreams could come true.

TERESA: Well, if whatever you dreamt helps you be a better pupil,
             it's all good with me.

RAHEEM: And I get why you might be a bit hard on me at times.
             You don't want anything to stand in the way of my dreams.
             I know I'm gonna have to work hard in life. After all,
             "life ain't no crystal stair".

(Teresa stands surprised at Raheem's comment.)

TERESA: You're right … "life ain't no crystal stair".

Martin Luther King's dream

"Every generation has somebody that sometimes has to make the ultimate sacrifice in order for people to get to the next level."

"I need you and America to have a better future, where it doesn't judge citizens by the colour of their skin."

"... there is a vast amount of people who, like us, want change. They hope for change, pray about change, eat change, drink change, sleep change and dream about change."

Raheem's dream

"I will never take for granted what people have done in this time ... so that I can dream any dream I want."

"... somehow I must carry on a torch that I didn't light. I must take the baton for a race I never entered."

"If everyone used History lessons to learn and make themselves a better person, then surely that would make a better world?"

Ideas for reading

Written by Clare Dowdall, PhD
Lecturer and Primary Literacy Consultant

Learning objectives: understand underlying themes, causes and points of view; recognise rhetorical devices used to persuade; sustain engagement with longer texts, using different techniques to make the text come alive; use a range of oral techniques to present persuasive arguments and engaging narratives

Curriculum links: History; Citizenship

Interest words: memorial, vision, prophesy, racists, generation, sacrifice, citizens, cynical, equality, segregation, civil rights, injustice, presidential, militant

Resources: whiteboard, images of Martin Luther King, ICT, internet

Getting started

This book can be read over two or more reading sessions.

- Look at the front cover together. Explain that the book is a playscript about a boy who is inspired by the daughter of Martin Luther King, the American civil rights activist and minister.

- Find out what the children already know about the Civil Rights Movement and Martin Luther King. List any information as a starting point for reading, e.g. he was a famous black man in America; he fought for the rights of black people; he made a speech that contained the famous words: *I have a dream*. Show children images of Martin Luther King to create a context for reading.

Reading and responding

- Turn to pp2–3. Introduce each character and establish that Raheem and Teresa are related, and that Martin Luther King and Yolanda are related. Ask children to take one character each and read through Scene 1 in pairs. Remind them of the conventions of playscripts, if necessary, e.g. stage directions.

- Ask children to discuss what they have learnt about Martin Luther King's character from reading Scene 1. Add their ideas to the list made earlier, e.g. he believed in non-violent protest; he was prepared to make a sacrifice for his cause.